D1292780

Read and Play
Fire Engines
by Jim Pipe

Stargazer Books
Mankato, Minnesota

fire engine

2

I am a
fire engine

3

crew

4

This is
my **crew**.

5

rush

6

I **rush** to a fire.

smoke

8

There is a lot of **smoke**.

9

fire

The **fire** is very hot.

hose

My **hoses**
carry water.

13

water

14

Water puts out the fire.

15

ladder

My **ladder**
goes high.

17

rescue

My crew go to the **rescue**!

19

What am I?

fire

ladder

hoses

crew

20

Match the words and pictures.

How many?

Can you count the fire crew?

On fire!

22 What is being used to fight these fires?

Index

23

For Parents and Teachers

Questions you could ask:

p. 2 Can you see the fire station? The fire station is where the firefighting equipment is stored and fire crews train. Some fire stations still have a pole that allows the crew to slide quickly down to the ground, where the fire engines are parked.

p. 4 What do firefighters wear? Thick, tough clothing protects them from the heat. Helmets protect their head from knocks, falling timber etc.

p. 6 What sound does a fire engine make? Encourage the reader to imitate the sound of a fire engine's siren when it is rushing to a fire.

p. 8 Why is smoke dangerous? Smoke can choke and even kill you. Firefighters carry equipment to help them breathe when there is thick smoke (see firefighter on page 8 with air canister and mask).

p. 10 Can you see the flames? Once a house catches fire the flames can spread fast; if a fire engine does not arrive soon it may burn down.

p. 13 Can you see the long hose? A fire engine pumps water along the hoses to the fire. The main hoses are up to 200 feet (60 meters) long and can gush water at 95 gallons (360 liters) a minute.

p. 16 How does a ladder help? It allows a fire crew to put out fires on tall buildings and to spray water from above. It can also be used to rescue people.

p. 18 What is the firefighter holding? He is using an axe to chop off a burning part of the building.

Activities you could do:

• Organize a visit to a local fire station to look at the fire engines and meet the fire crew.

• Role play: ask the reader to act out being a firefighter, e.g. sliding down pole, driving fire engine, using hoses to spray water on the fire, climbing up ladder, and cutting through door.

• Play Chinese Whispers: an "Emergency" message such as "the cat is stuck in the tree" is whispered by one child to the next until the message returns to the start. How much has it changed?

© Aladdin Books Ltd 2009

Designed and produced by
Aladdin Books Ltd

First published in 2009 in the United States by
Stargazer Books,
distributed by
Black Rabbit Books
PO Box 3263
Mankato, MN 56002

Library of Congress Cataloging-in-Publication Data

Pipe, Jim, 1966-
  Fire engines / Jim Pipe.
    p. cm. -- (Read and play)
  Includes bibliographical references and index.
  Summary: "In very simple language and photographs, describes fire engines. Includes quizzes and games"--Provided by publisher.
   ISBN 978-1-59604-177-6
  1. Fire engines--Juvenile literature. I. Title.
  TH9372.P57 2009
  628.9'259--dc22
                2008015283

Series consultant
Zoe Stillwell is an experienced preschool teacher.

Photocredits:
l-left, r-right, b-bottom, t-top, c-center, m-middle
All photos from istockphoto.com except: 16-17, 20tl—Christopher Jensen/Dreamstime.